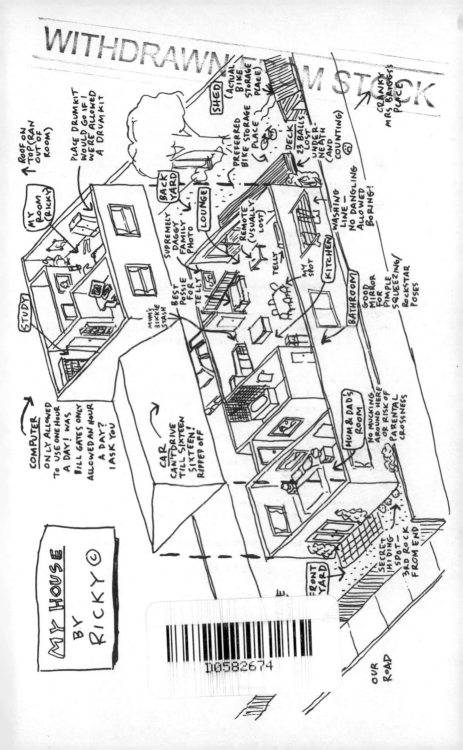

STORY ONE

FALLING
FOR IT

1
SEEING THINGS

SOME THINGS YOU SHOULD KNOW ABOUT **ME.**

- Freckles. I once joined them up like a dot-to-dot, but they didn't make a picture. I just got a face covered in pen.

- I go red when I get embarrassed, angry, sad, hot, happy, busting to go to the toilet, and probably other things I haven't discovered yet. It's totally embarrassing (which makes me go even redder).

- Uncool brain.

- Favourite stripy t-shirt. Grandad called me 'The Zebra'.

- Shorts. Even in winter. Mum says I'm weird.

- Sneakers. Probably the wrong brand.

People think I am weird. Even Mum (although she is nice about it). The kids at school basically avoid me. I spend most of recess hanging around on my own.

The other kids don't see things the same way as me. I spend a lot of time imagining.

I just don't get it. Inside my head I am not the same as other kids.

Like for example, once, our teacher Jenny took us all out onto the oval and told us to lie on our backs on the grass.

'Look up at the clouds,' she said. 'Tell me what you see.'

We all stared up at the clouds in silence. There was so much up there. It was like a circus on a busy day.

Sean Green spoke up. 'I see a duck,' he said.

'There's a car,' said Mahood.

'I see a little bunny,' said Mandy Chow.

'They are all very good imaginings,' said Jenny.

'What about you, Ricky? What do you see?'

I told them what I saw.

'There is a horse,' I said. 'It stands twenty-two hands high. A stallion, wild and free. The smaller clouds are the other horses. They follow him *every*where – they follow him *any*where. His name is Thundercloud.'

I was excited by the clouds. I went on, telling everyone what I saw.

'Thundercloud has never been tamed,' I said. 'He leads his mob over the mountains. One flick of his tail can make lightning. His eyes are like burning coals from hell.'

When I had finished there was a long silence.

After a bit, Jenny said, 'That's very good, Ricky.'

No one else thought so.

Mandy Chow pointed to another cloud. 'I see a lovely little bunny,' she said. 'Ricky's horse sucks.'

She glared at me with half-closed eyes. She didn't like me. No one seems to like me much. Especially girls. I don't know why.

Our teacher smiled at me.

'Do you see anything else, Ricky?' she asked.

I did.

'Weirdo,' said Mandy Chow.

I just don't get it.

What did I do wrong?

It was just a cloud.

2

TRYING FLYING

Here is a list of things I am good at. A cross means no good. A tick means excellent.

Being a dork gets a tick because that's what I am.

There is one more thing I get a tick for on my self-report card. Oh, yes, I get a tick for flying. And that's because I can.

It started when I was a little kid.

I used to leap off anything I could find.

I wanted to fly.

I wanted to be up there with the birds, soaring around in the clouds and taking in the view. But I didn't just want to fly – I wanted everyone to see me fly. I guess you could say I was nutty about it.

I wanted people to point up and say, 'Look at Ricky. He's flying.' I wanted their eyes to bug out. I wanted them to faint with surprise.

I wanted to be ...

Nothing ever happened though. Every time
I jumped, I just dropped back to the ground.

So I tried it from the shed roof. I thought, 'Believe
in yourself, Ricky.'

Dad was always saying, 'Go for it, Ricky. Nothing
ever happens unless you take a risk.'

I climbed on top of the wall around our back garden and up onto the roof of Dad's shed.

It was a long way down. I closed my eyes, yelled out, 'Go Ricky,' at the top of my voice and leapt forward with outstretched hands.

After I got out of hospital I decided on a new approach.

I tried using the power of my mind to lift myself up – levitation. I would screw up my eyes and try to fly just by thinking about it. I would imagine my feet slowly rising as I chanted. 'Fly, fly, fly.'

It didn't work. But I didn't give up. Every day I would try again. 'Fly, fly, fly.'

Mum thought I was crazy.

Don't get me wrong. I love her. She is the best mum in the world and she mostly just rolls her eyes when she sees me trying to fly.

Once I was in the kitchen trying to fly. I screwed up my eyes and concentrated. I tried to lift my feet off the floor. Just by brain power.

'Fly, fly, fly,' I said aloud.

At that very moment Mum walked in. 'What are you doing?' she said.

'I'm trying to lift my feet off the ground. I want to fly. Up in the air.'

Mum looked worried. 'Have you talked to your father about this?' she said.

'I'm not strange,' I yelled. 'Dad said you can do anything if you try hard enough.'

'Well, not everything,' said Mum.

'Is he a liar?'

'No, he just gets carried away.'

'I believe him,' I said. 'I'm going to fly.'

'I don't think that's a good idea,' said Mum.

'I'll bet you fifty dollars,' I said.

'You haven't got fifty dollars,' said Mum.

Mum has an answer for everything. It's annoying.

I waggled my finger at her like she does sometimes. 'Dad always says, "Put your money where your mouth is."'

'No,' she said. 'I'm not going to bet. Instead of trying to fly, why don't you try to clean up your room?'

'For ten dollars?' I said.

'For nothing,' said Mum. 'It's your room.'

'I'm saving up to go to Water World and ride on the Super Sucker Water Slide,' I said. 'Every kid in my class has been to Water World except me.'

Mum snorted. 'I must have heard that one about a million times before,' she said. 'But I'll tell you what. If you stop this silly business of trying to fly I'll take you to Water World.'

I thought about it. I thought about it really hard. But I knew that one day I would fly. 'No thanks,' I said.

'Okay, then,' said Mum. 'If you clean up your room every day for six months I'll take you to Water World.'

I thought about this offer for a long time. But I shook my head. The price was just too high. Even for a visit to Water World and a ride on the Super Sucker. I couldn't clean my bedroom every morning for six months. I just couldn't do it. Mum looked at me in a worried way and gave a big sigh.

I went up to my room and read my favourite comic.

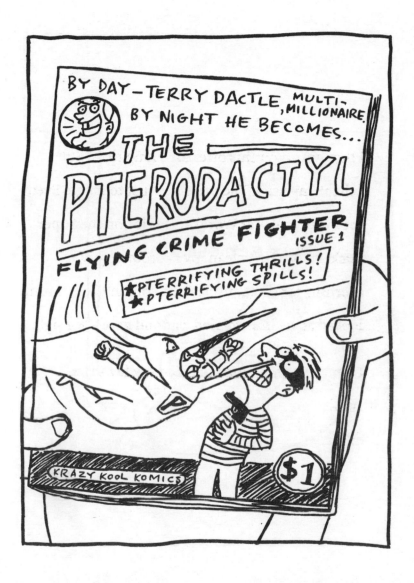

3

LIFTING OFF

I freaked out. I was really doing it.

I was floating in the air above the beanbag.

I screamed.

Then I smiled. And laughed. I could do it.

I could really do it. I was flying.

'Woo hoo,' I yelled. 'Look at me. Look at me.
I can fly.'

Feet pounded down the hall.

Mum ran into the room, closely followed by Dad.

'What? What? What?' yelled Mum.

'I flew. I flew. Did you see it?'

'I saw you jump into the beanbag, Ricky,'
said Mum.

She had that worried look on her face. She must
have thought I was losing my marbles.

'No, no, I flew.'

'Don't try to fly,' said Mum. 'Join the football team
or something sensible.'

'No. I did, I did it, I flew,' I shouted. 'Watch this.'

Mum sighed.

'Fly, fly, fly,' I said to myself. 'Lift off. Feet rise up.'

'Stop it,' said Mum. 'You will do yourself an injury.'

'I did fly,' I said. But even as I said the words

I started to have doubts. Was it a dream?

Was I going nuts? Did I really lift off the ground?

'I did fly,' I said. 'My feet…' The words trailed away.

'I always wished I could fly, too,' Dad said quietly.

'Really?' I asked.

He nodded.

'Yes,' said Mum. 'And look what happened.'

'What do you mean?' I said.

'Don't,' said Dad. But Mum tightened her lips, then kept talking.

'It was when you were just a baby, Ricky. You know Mrs Briggs over the fence?'

'Old Mrs Briggs?'

'Yes. Her kitten got stuck up the flagpole in the front yard. She was crying something terrible and there was no one there to help. Except Dad. Mrs Briggs rushed inside to call the fire brigade and while she was gone Dad sprang into action.'

I stared at Dad with pride. 'You climbed a flagpole to save a kitten? You are a hero, Dad.'

Dad blushed.

'Except,' said Mum, 'that when Mrs Briggs came outside...'

'Don't,' said Dad.

Mum didn't take any notice of Dad blushing. She just went on with the story.

'And your father was stuck up on top of the pole. He couldn't get down.'

'That's enough, Mary,' said Dad. 'He doesn't want to know all this.'

'Yes, I do,' I said.

Mum kept going. 'Everyone in the street came to look. There he was – a grown man clinging to the top of a flagpole. By the time the fire brigade came to save him there were hundreds of people watching.'

'Wow,' I said. Dad gave a little groan.

'We were a laughing stock. That cat saved itself and climbed down the pole. And your father got stuck. The whole country knew that he climbed a flagpole and couldn't get down. That's how well he could fly.'

She gave a little smile and then she added. 'But I still love him.'

'So do I,' I said.

I do too. Dad's a bit strange. But then, so am I.

Birds of a feather. That's us.

4

LIKE A BIRD

The next morning I put on my backpack and walked slowly to school. I went through the park so that I could try once more. I wanted to see if I could lift myself off the ground again with only the power of thought.

But I didn't want anyone to see me going red in the face and groaning with the effort.

I stopped halfway across the park and sat on a bench. I thought about how amazing it would be to fly high up in the sky, not just a metre above a beanbag. I knew it would be fantastic. Up there like a bird.

I stood and checked out the park.

'Fly, fly, fly,' I said under my breath.

My ears grew hot. My eyes throbbed.

Slowly, slowly, I rose into the air.

Now I needed someone to see me. Now I needed someone to almost faint at the sight of my amazing powers. 'Look at me,' I shouted.

No one heard me. I yelled louder.

'I'm flying, I'm flying.'

The words had no sooner left my mouth than I fell. I plopped straight down to the ground.

I closed my eyes and tried again. I strained and strained, but nothing happened.

I walked along the winding path. One more try. I would give it one more go. There was nothing I wanted more than to get to school and show off my flying ability.

I concentrated really hard. And once again it happened. I looked around, but there was no one in sight.

The word 'forward' sprang into my mind. Slowly I began to move along the path hovering a few centimetres above the ground. 'Higher,' I thought. I rose about fifty centimetres more. I was floating along the path and my feet weren't even touching the ground.

This was amazing. This was fantastic. Awesome.
It was like skating on ice except there was nothing
under my feet but air.

I flew around a tree. I flew over a rubbish bin.
I felt as if my body was filled with helium. It was
absolutely mind-blowing.

'Hey,' the gardener yelled. 'Can't you read?

Get off the grass, you little brat.'

I tried to make sense of it. Sometimes I could
fly and sometimes I couldn't. I needed to show
someone. I needed someone to believe me.
Then everything would be okay.

A far off beeping noise sounded through the trees.
It was the school bell. I was going to be late.

'Up,' I thought. Up I went. Not high. Just a little
off the ground.

'Forward,' I thought. I flew forward.

'Faster,' I thought. I went faster.

I didn't say the words aloud. I didn't have to.
I just thought them. Brain power was enough.

Faster and faster I sped through the park, standing straight up and skidding forward like a bishop on a chess board. The feeling of speed and power and lightness was fantastic. I was dizzy with happiness.

I sped along in silence. My heart was thumping. This was my big chance. Everyone was going to see me fly. I would be a dork no longer. I would be the amazing flying boy. The school gate came into view.

There were kids gathered around staring at something on the ground. No one was looking at me. Except…

The little girl shook her head. She wasn't sure what she had just seen. She joined the other kids who were all staring down into the ground. There was orange netting surrounding a deep hole where workers had been digging for several days.

But there were no workers. Only kids.

'What's going on?' I said. No one answered me,
so I looked for myself.

5

IN A HOLE

The poor little dog had fallen down the hole and was unconscious at the bottom. The little girl started to cry. It was a very deep hole.

'Poor little doggy,' she said.

Suddenly a voice sounded behind us. 'Into school everyone. Quick. We will call the fire brigade.'

It was our teacher, Jenny. She picked up the little girl and headed for the school office.

Everyone shuffled away. Everyone except me.

I was alone at the edge of the hole.

'Up,' I said.

I floated up.

'Forward.' Now I was hovering over the hole.
This was scary. It was a long drop to the bottom.

'Down,' I said.

I began to descend.

Down,

     down,

          down.

It was dark and cold. I landed gently on my feet.

The dog was lying on its side with its eyes closed.

I picked it up and cradled it in my arms.

'Up,' I said.

Up I went. Up, up, up – nearly halfway.

Then...

Whoosh. Crash. Splash. I hit the muddy bottom.

With a thump. My ankle was twisted and every

bone in my body jarred. I groaned in agony.

The little dog was still cradled in my arms.

I could hear shouting and yelling from above.

What was happening? What made me fall?

Suddenly it clicked.

'I get it,' I said to the dog. 'Now I see.'

I took off my backpack and tipped out my books.

I had to be quick. There was muffled barking,

but I ignored it.

'Up.'

Slowly I floated up. I stopped when my head was just below the top. I closed my eyes and gave myself an instruction. 'Up, over the edge and down.' That's what I thought. And that's exactly what happened.

A group of teachers were hurrying across the yard. But all they saw was a boy plopping out of the hole with a dog.

Jenny took the dog from my arms and pulled my backpack off its head. The other teachers peered down the hole. There was nothing there but muddy books.

'How did you do that?'

'It's five metres deep.'

'Impossible.'

'The kid's a mountain goat.'

'A monkey more like it.'

They were all patting me on the back.

'You should have waited,' said Jenny. 'It was dangerous. How did you climb out of there?'

'I flew,' I said.

The teachers laughed.

'He has a sense of humour too.'

So I was a hero. Sort of. They called me to the stage at school assembly. I was told off for climbing down the hole because it was dangerous. And I was praised for bravery and climbing skills. Everyone was nice to me.

But no one believed I could fly.

6

TELLING DAD

Dad was waiting for me after comics club at school. As I limped home I told him the whole story. The true story. Even though I knew he wouldn't believe it.

We sat down on a bench just over the road from the town hall. The Australian flag flew from a pole right up on the top. It was growing late and a man was pulling the flag down. He wrapped it up and went inside.

'I know you don't believe me,' I said to Dad. 'But I can fly.'

Dad had a serious expression on his face. 'How do you feel about that?' he said.

Why did Dad say that? It's the sort of thing the school counsellor asks. Why couldn't he just believe me? I mean, I was a hero.

I thought for a bit. 'It's lonely,' I said. 'No one else can do it. Not one person in the whole world. There's no one to talk to about it. No one to share the fun. Or the scary bits. No one to help or give advice. No one knows what I can do.'

Dad nodded, but didn't say anything. He didn't even seem to be listening.

But I had so many thoughts that I just kept talking.

'There are lots of people in the world who know what their gift is. They play violins or lay bricks. Everyone knows what they can do. There are people who build houses or climb mountains and they can all talk to each other about it. But I am the only one who can fly. The only one. And no one believes me. Not even Mum. Or you.'

Dad stared at the footpath. Finally he spoke.

'Close your eyes.'

'What?'

He looked along the empty street. 'Just do it. Close your eyes and count to ten.'

I did as he said.

'Up here.' Dad's voice sounded far away.

I opened my eyes, but I couldn't see him. I looked above my head. Still nothing. Then I stared at the top of the town hall.

'How did you…?'

'Close your eyes and count again,' he yelled.

I tried to keep my eyes closed, but when I got
to five, they just flew open.

Dad was still coming down, like an upright soldier
being lowered with invisible hands.
He was about two metres above the ground.
As soon as I saw him, he fell like a garbage bag full
of rocks.

'Ouch,' he screamed as he hit the footpath.

'Dad,' I shouted. 'Sorry, I looked too soon.'

He stood up and dusted himself down. There was a moment of silence. Then he smiled at me.

'Just make sure you never let anyone see you with your feet off the ground,' he said.

I grinned and we both laughed.

'Life is good,' I said to Dad. 'It's fantastic being able to fly, but I want people to see me doing it. I wish they could. I really do.'

I let my mind wander. If the kids at school could see me flying I would be a superhero. Just thinking about it made me happy.

One day my dreams would come true.
I just knew it.

'Make another wish,' said Dad.

I did.

And Mum made it happen.

STORY TWO

THE KANGAPOO KEY RING

1

GROWING PAINS

'**I** wish it was still alive,' said Mum with a sigh.

I stared at the picture on the wall. A picture of something special. Something that once belonged to Grandad.

I shook my head sadly. 'Me too,' I said. 'Then we would be rich.'

'Don't think like that,' said Mum. 'Money isn't everything. He was a good father to me. That's the main thing.'

Grandad had promised to leave Mum a gift that was worth a lot of money. His rare black-petal poppy plant. It was the only one in the world. Grandad had spent years developing it.

The poppy was worth a fortune. He wished he had more, but he only had one. He dreamed of growing hundreds of the plants and making a lot of money. So he could leave it to Mum. For her to buy microwaves when they busted. And maybe a swimming pool. And an electric guitar.

Mum's eyes started to water.

She wiped away a tear. 'I can't bear to think about what happened,' she said. 'Grandad made a mistake. He left the pot plant out in the backyard. The only black-petal poppy in the world.'

I shook my head. I knew the rest of the story. The rabbits ate every bit of the poppy – the flowers, the leaves, the stem, the seed pods. Everything.

'Why don't you grow some more?' I said.

Mum sighed. 'I've told you before. We don't know how. The secret died with Grandad.'

Grandad was weird. But I couldn't say that to Mum. Not now he was dead. He had a plan, but a rabbit ruined it. He was just a dreamer. Like me.

SOME THINGS YOU SHOULD KNOW ABOUT **GRANDAD**.

- A joker. Always laughing.
- Hair often used in place of a napkin.
- Little veins in nose.
- Had a huge collection of funny sayings like 'It's going off like a frog in a sock'.
- Had a walking stick called Sticky.
- Made pictures by gluing his own toenail clippings onto paper (true!)

Grandad's toenail pictures weren't worth anything.

Dad said they were revolting rubbish.

But the poppy wasn't rubbish. If Mum had that

she could have been rich. But now she was poor.

If only I could help. If I could grow a black-petal

poppy we would make a mint. But I couldn't.

There was only one thing I was good at.

Flying.

That was it.

I could make a lot of money by flying around.

People would pay good money to see a flying boy.

I went into the lounge. Dad was asleep in front

of the TV. I woke him up.

'Dad,' I said. 'I know you don't want me to, but

I need to fly. And I need people to see me.'

Dad frowned. He was cross with me. He looked

upwards and then checked to see that Mum

was busy.

'The roof,' he said. 'Right now. I'll join you when

the coast is clear.'

2

SEEING THINGS

Dad and I sat on the edge of the roof.

We lived in a two-storey house and it was a long way down to the ground. We must have looked like Santa Claus and his helper perched up there in the middle of the night. And like Santa, no one was allowed to see us.

'Don't even think of it,' said Dad. 'If anyone sees you flying, you will drop like a stone. And once you start to fall nothing can save you. Even if the person stops looking.'

'Dogs too,' I said. 'That dog I was telling you about stared at me when I was flying out of the well. And then…whoo.'

'And cats,' said Dad thoughtfully. He seemed to be remembering something he would rather forget.

'What about rabbits?' I asked.

'I'm not sure about rabbits,' Dad said. 'They don't look up much.'

'Cows?'

'Cows are really bad. You could be flying high

across a paddock and a heap of cows look up.'

'Rats?'

'No,' said Dad.

'Mice?'

'Nah, they nick off at the first sign of a shadow. They think you might be a hawk or some other bird of prey.'

'Birds?'

'Birds are really dangerous.'

'Worms?'

We both laughed. 'Worms don't have eyes,'
said Dad.

'Are there any other animals we need to be careful
around?'

'Yes,' said Dad. 'One is especially dangerous. The
most dangerous animal on earth.'

'Humans?' I whispered.

'Yes,' said Dad. 'They are curious. And they have

binoculars. And they fly in aeroplanes. And

remember, all it takes is one glimpse and down

you will go. All the way to the ground.'

He looked at me seriously. 'That's why I've brought

you up here. No one must ever see you

fly. A boy flying is something weird. If you are

seen once, everyone will be looking for you.

They will try to find the Flying Boy. Or should I say,

Falling Boy.

'And you must promise me that you won't fly more than a few centimetres above the ground. No high flying.'

Dad went silent, waiting for me to promise. Instead I asked a question.

'If no one can see you...' I said slowly. 'If no one knows...'

'Yes?'

'What's the point of it? There's no glory. No show. I mean, you and me are the only people in the world who can fly. But what's the use of it if everyone thinks we are just ordinary?'

'Ordinary is okay,' said Dad.

'Not for me it isn't,' I said. 'I want to be...

Dad frowned at me.

'What's wrong with that?' I asked.

Dad paused again. 'At your age,' he said, 'nothing.
But I can tell you from experience that you don't
need fame to be happy. Now promise me that you
won't fly more than a couple of centimetres off the
ground.'

'Let's go down,' I said.

Dad sighed, then smiled. He checked to see if the coast was clear. The backyard and the street were bathed in moonlight.

We waited until a cloud drifted in front of the moon.

'Now,' said Dad. 'Go, go, go.'

He shut his eyes so that he couldn't see me.

I concentrated.

After I landed I stared up at Dad and then closed my eyes. 'Your turn,' I yelled.

'Dad flying,' he yelled.

'Dad flying,' I replied as I shut my eyes.

There was a soft thud on the ground next to me as Dad landed.

'I'm tired,' I said.

Dad nodded. 'Flying is hard work. Keeping your body off the ground uses up energy. Even your clothes are heavy. So don't go trying to lift things when you fly.'

I didn't get to practise flying much the next day because something else was going on.

Mum was sad. Because of Grandad. He was gone now. He died of a heart attack from laughing at one of his own jokes.

But today Mum wasn't laughing. It was two years since Grandad died. A tear ran down her face as she stared at the only thing she had to remember him by.

A present he gave her just before he cracked his final joke.

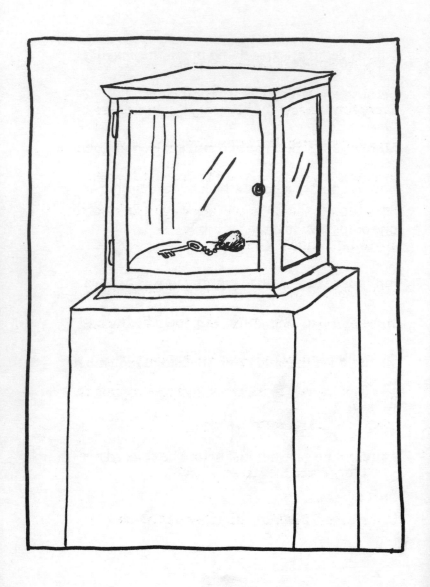

A key ring made of kangaroo poo.

Every time he saw the key ring, Dad rolled his eyes and snorted. But Mum loved it. She kept it in a glass case which I wasn't allowed to touch. Even though the kangapoo key ring wasn't worth anything, Mum loved it.

Mum pointed to the glass case. 'Grandad was always playing jokes,' she said. 'Who else would make a key ring with a piece of kangaroo poo glued on the end of it? The kangapoo key ring is all we have to remind us of him.'

'Don't forget the toenail art,' I said.

Dad snorted. But Mum didn't seem to hear.

That night I lay in bed thinking. I bet that key

opened something special.

If I could find it, I would make Mum the happiest person in the world. It would make up for the money she didn't get because the rabbits ate the poppy.

Mum never complained about money, but we didn't have much. We still had an old computer and the microwave was busted.

'You don't need money to be happy,' she often said.

All the same, she sometimes looked sad when we couldn't afford takeaway on Friday nights.

WHAT I WOULD GET MUM IF WE HAD MONEY

©RICKY

- Decent running shoes.
- Trip to some island with palm trees.
- Buy some island with palm trees.
- Fix bathroom up.
- The best takeaway
- Fix bathroom up again.
- Big Van Gogh painting for living room. Little one for the loo.
  - Personal assistant.

There were boxes of old stuff at the back of the garden shed. What if I could find a locked box that the key fitted? Something Mum and Dad had missed. I would be a hero. Especially if I found something worth a lot of money.

But I had to be careful. If anything happened to the key ring I would be history.

3

THE JOKER

I switched my phone to torch mode.

Then I put on my tracksuit and crept downstairs. I tiptoed along the hall and into the kitchen. The glass case sparkled in the light from my phone.

I went outside and hurried across the wet grass

towards the shed. The rain was already making my

shoulders wet so I broke into a run.

Splash. Down I went.

Rats. I staggered to my feet. I was wet and cold.
My warm bed was calling to me. Stupid, stupid,
stupid. Why hadn't I waited until Mum and Dad
were out shopping? Then I could search in the
daylight.

I opened the creaking door.

The light from my phone shone on the shed's
dusty secrets.

At one end I saw Dad's tools and crazy inventions.
At the other end I saw cardboard boxes, cobwebs,
nuts and bolts, broken furniture and useless bits
and pieces.

I was looking for something that was actually nothing.

A hole.

A keyhole.

I put my hand into my tracksuit-top pocket.

Nothing.

There was nothing there.

It was gone. I patted myself all over in panic.

The kangapoo key ring was gone. And so was I.

I was dead meat.

Mum would never forgive me if I had lost the

precious key ring. I must have dropped it when

I slipped in the puddle. My heart thumped in

my chest.

The puddle was shallow. But all I could feel was grass and water. Suddenly something glinted in the light of my phone. I grabbed it. Oh, yes, yes, yes. It was the key ring. I could hardly believe my luck.

My bad luck.

The piece of kangaroo poo was gone. I groped

around desperately in the freezing water. Nothing.

Nothing. Nothing. Then my fingers felt a piece

of slimy mush. It was just a smear, a smidgen of

a smudge. It was all that was left of the kangaroo

poo. I rinsed my fingers in the icy puddle and

made my way to the back door with the poo-less

key ring.

In the morning I would have to face Mum. She would never forgive me. Grandad's key ring was ruined. It was just a joke key ring. But now it was a bad joke. A very bad joke. A kangapoo key ring with no poo.

My thoughts raced. What if I could find another piece of kangaroo poo?

The only problem was there there weren't any kangaroos around here anymore. In the old days there were plenty. But now the bush was gone. Gobbled up by houses.

I stood in the back garden with the rain pelting down on my head. I was soaked. I was shivering. I was desperate.

Suddenly an idea popped into my head. Yes, yes, yes. I couldn't get the poo back, but I could still save myself.

But first I had to get back to my bedroom without waking Mum and Dad.

4

PERFECT COPY

I looked up at my bedroom window.

Then I quickly checked out the back garden. No one would see me. I concentrated. Nothing happened. My wet clothes were heavy. I tried harder.

Slowly my feet left the ground. Up, up, up. I rose to the second storey and until I reached my bedroom window. Then I flew gently inside and plopped onto the floor.

I shut the window and took off my wet clothes.

I dried myself and put on my pyjamas. Then

I turned on my bedroom light and pulled open the

top drawer of my desk.

I was looking for something that I could make into

fake kangaroo poo.

Blu Tack. Yes, yes, yes.

I rolled a small piece of the rubbery strip into

a ball and pressed it onto the end of the key ring

chain. Perfect.

Except for one thing.

It was blue. Sky blue. Kangaroo poo was definitely not found in shades of blue.

Then I had a brainwave. I grinned. 'Ricky boy,' I said to myself. 'You are a genius.'

I knelt down and ran my finger over the floor under my bed. Perfect. I rolled the Blu Tack in the dust. Good move. It was just the right colour – kangapoo brown.

I tiptoed downstairs and put the key ring back in its glass case.

I wondered if Mum would notice the fake poo. If she did I was in BIG TROUBLE. Poor Mum. Now I had two secrets to keep from her. I wished I could tell her that I could fly, but Dad wouldn't allow it. And now I had glued fake poo on her beloved key ring.

I felt a bit guilty.

The next day Mum took the key ring out of its special case.

But she didn't notice a thing. Another day passed. Then a week. Then a month. I had got away with it.

Sometimes Mum would stare out into the backyard and look a little sad. I knew that she was thinking about the black-petal poppy. I knew that she would give a million key rings for the secret of that plant. She would be able to grow hundreds of them and make enough money to get the bathroom fixed up.

She was really down in the dumps. How could I cheer her up?

I suddenly had an amazing thought. Why didn't
I think of it before? Grandad had spent years
mucking around with different poppies. He knew
about DNA and grafting and cross-fertilising
and all that stuff. He had probably written the
secret down somewhere. On a piece of paper. And
hidden it in a locked box or tin.

Yes, yes, yes.

No man in his right mind would make a joke
kangapoo key ring unless the key fitted something.
Something important. The poppy's secret was in
a box. And I bet the box was still in the shed.

I would have to try again.

5

BIRD BRAIN

Once more I waited until Mum and Dad were asleep.

Still in my pyjamas I crept downstairs.

I heard a noise. It was Dad going to the loo.

I nipped back up to my room. I heard the toilet

flush and then voices in the lounge room. He'd

turned the TV on. He probably couldn't sleep.

'Okay,' I said to myself. 'I'll fly down to the shed.'

I carefully put the key ring on the windowsill

and took off my pyjamas. It was cold outside so

I would have to put on my warmest clothes.

I stood there totally naked trying to work out what to wear. That's when I saw a scary sight.

It was one of those moments when you know something terrible is going to happen. And it will happen so fast that you won't be able to stop it. Your whole life hangs on that moment. Nothing will ever be the same again. And you just can't do a thing about it.

Time froze. The owl blinked. It only took a split

second. But it seemed like an hour. An hour in

which I was made of rock.

It blinked again and then…oh, no. Oh, horror.

No, no, no. The owl picked up the key ring in its

beak, flapped its wings and flew off into the night.

My body shivered. I was still naked. I hesitated.

Then I did the only thing I could do.

I was as naked as a plucked chook. And as

cold as a frozen one. My fingers were already

numb. I should have turned back. I should have

flown home. But I couldn't. I had to get that key

ring back.

Through the swirling mist I could just see the

owl. Its wings flapped lazily. I had no wings.

Only the force of my own mind to hold me aloft.

I had never flown this fast before. Or this far.

The owl was gliding, but every now and then it flapped and rose a metre or so. How high would it go? How high would I go?

I realised I was in terrible danger. When I flew out of my window I had acted by instinct. I hadn't stopped to think. What if the moon came out? What if someone saw my white skin glaring against the black night? Or what if the owl turned and looked at me? I would plunge to the ground and die.

The owl was just a bird. And I was a bird brain.

I didn't want to die. Not before the whole world

could see me fly high in the sky.

High?

Oh, no. Somewhere way below me was the ground.

I was naked and the cold air was biting my fingers

and toes and nipping at my... oh, no.

I couldn't see the owl. I couldn't see anything.

I was flying blind. Something scratched my bare

stomach. Twigs. Leaves. There were trees beneath

me. All around me.

I heard the owl hoot. Its boo-book sound

disturbed the silence of the forest. But I wasn't

interested.

I forgot about the kangapoo key ring. I forgot about the black-petal poppy. All I could think about was getting to the ground safely. I was in deadly danger. A grey light was already washing the horizon. The sun was coming up. Distant clouds were turning pink. A car sounded in the distance. And then another.

People. People were down there. People with

eyes to see me. The ground was still a black

nothingness beneath me. I lowered myself. Gently,

gently, gently. The icy leaves of another tree

brushed my naked skin. Then another and another.

I could sense that I was approaching the earth.

I was in free air. But what lay beneath me?

Terrible visions filled my head.

The clouds were beginning to glow. I had to get home before dawn. But I was naked and soon it would be light. Even if I flew through the gloom someone might see my pale, bare body. I could fly low to the ground and then if I fell, at least it wouldn't be much of a fall. But I had another problem. An even bigger one.

I was freezing cold. My body was covered in

goosebumps. If didn't find some clothes I could

die of exposure.

Two round discs appeared in the shadows

of an unseen tree. Bright yellow discs. Eyes.

The owl had seen me.

6

ON THE ROAD

NEXT 10 kms

Sploosh. Down I went. It was only a small drop to the ground. I had landed safely.

But my feet had plunged into something squishy. And stinky. Where was I?

A low deep moan filled the night air. And filled me with terror. A loud groan sounded. And then another. The moans and groans were mournful, like foghorns in the ghostly night.

A dark shape with horns loomed through the mist.

A demon of the dark.

'Aaagh,' I screamed.

The monster jumped back and ran off with an uneven gallop. Filthy wet goo squirted out of its backside. A cow. A stupid cow.

The cold breeze made me shiver. The remains of my fear made me shake. Every part of me was freezing cold.

Except my feet.

My mind went into overdrive.

Yes, yes, yes. The answer to all my problems.

I bent down and picked up a handful of the warm, wet, stinking dung. I gagged at the stench, but the warmth seeped through my skin.

'Oh, wonderful,' I said to myself. 'Happiness is warm cow dung.'

I stared at the warm goo in my hand. Could I do it? No, no, no.

I took a deep breath.

Oh, it was wonderful.

Oh, it was terrible.

I covered my whole body in cow dung.

I was now a lovely shade of brown – cow-poo brown. It was the perfect way to hide my skin. The ultimate camouflage. And it was warm. It would save my life.

It was kangaroo poo that got me into this mess. And it was cow poo that was going to get me out of it.

I rose a half a metre above the grassy paddock and flew forward. I swept over the field wearing my brown coat of many smells. No one would see me until the sun rose. But I had to hurry.

Without warning a bright beam of light swept the paddock and disappeared. A car's engine roared and then slowly faded in the distance.

There was a road nearby. I could follow it home.

I floated along the grassy verge. Every time a car approached I lowered myself to the ground. I must have looked like the statue of some ancient god standing guard at the side of the road. Or perhaps I just resembled a tree trunk. No one stopped.

The sky grew lighter and I knew that I did not have long to go until curious eyes would put a stop to my flight.

I increased speed and flew as fast as I could just above the grass. The ground sped by in a blur.

PROBLEMS WITH COATING YOURSELF IN COW MANURE

LOOK LIKE
A GIANT POO

NOT ACTUALLY
WARM FOR THAT
LONG

THE
SMELL

SOON
ITCHY

HARDENS AND CRACKS
OFF AFTER A WHILE

COWS LOOK
AT YOU FUNNY

I started to shiver again just as the first rays of

sunlight peeped over the horizon. In the growing

light I could see that I was in open farmland.

Not a tree was in sight. But I could tell from the

scattered farm houses that I was close to town.

Not far from home.

Hurry. Hurry. Hurry.

My smelly brown cloak was still keeping out

the worst of the cold and was great camouflage.

Then the sky grew blacker. The rays of sun

disappeared. A blustery wind arose. I had to

work hard at staying on course.

And then it began.

At first just a few specks. Then heavy drops. Soon it was pelting down. Cow dung dribbled down my legs and ran off my shoulders. Desperately I tried to smear the dung over the white patches of skin that were appearing as the rain washed me clean.

The wind was blowing me off course. I had to do something or I would be seen.

Anyone coming along this road would notice me for sure. A naked, flying boy.

I dropped to the ground and plastered the few

remaining smears of cow dung over my most

embarrassing parts.

The sound of a car's engine crept up on me.

'Look, it's him,' screamed a woman's voice.

I tried to cover my nakedness.

'Don't worry,' said the voice. 'You haven't got anything I haven't seen before.'

'Mum,' I shouted. I rushed over and hugged her. She had tears in her eyes.

'What's the matter?' I said.

She looked down at her wet, poo-stained dressing gown. Her expression changed from relief to... something else.

'Get in the car,' Dad said quickly.

I was saved.

Or was I?

'You smell of cow poo,' said Mum. 'Try not to get it on the seats.'

On the way home I explained about chasing after the key ring. And how I found it, but it was ruined. I didn't say anything about flying of course. Mum must never know. She grew frostier and frostier.

'You were told not to touch that key ring,' she said.

I didn't tell her about the kangaroo poo falling off it into the puddle in our garden. Now it was gone there was no point.

'We'll talk about this more when you are warm and dry,' she said. 'And you can tell me why you are naked.'

I felt guilty. The key ring had gone the way of the black-petal poppy. Now Mum had nothing to remind her of Grandad.

7

A SORT OF SMILE

Mum sure was mad about the lost key ring.

'The only thing I had of Grandad's,' she said.

'I was just trying to find the secret of the black-petal poppy,' I said. 'So that we could grow some more and buy a new microwave and computer.'

'Yes,' said Dad. 'That's true. Maybe we're being a bit harsh.'

Mum shook her head and looked down at her shoes.

I walked over to the window and stared at the rain that was still pelting down. Mum was looking at the worn sofa and the faded curtains. And the heater that was turned off because we couldn't afford the electricity.

'If only rabbits hadn't eaten the poppy,' said Mum. 'Our troubles would be over. I know Grandad grew it as a gift for me. So that we could all have a better life.'

Then I saw something outside in the garden.

At first I didn't believe it. But it was true.

Yes, yes, yes. Amazing.

'Are you sure it was rabbits that ate the black-petal
poppy?' I shouted.

'What else would it be?' said Mum.

'A kangaroo,' I yelled.

Mum and Dad stared at me.

'I dropped the kangaroo poo in that puddle,' I said.

'The poo must have had seeds from the poppy

in it.'

Life is strange. Who would have thought that

a kangaroo had eaten the black-petal poppy?

Who would have thought that Grandad would find

a piece of kangaroo poo from the same animal?

And glue it on the end of a key ring?

The seeds inside the poo had grown in the puddle

where I dropped it. I was a hero in my own home.

Just by luck.

Mum couldn't stop kissing me which was a bit embarrassing. Dad flapped his arms like a bird and winked. I was off the hook.

That night I took a big risk. I put on some shorts and a T-shirt and flew back to the tree where I had seen the owl. Its nest was empty except for a few rat bones and...

I grabbed the key ring and flew quickly back home.

I looked at the key ring. And the key. It must

open something. But what?

 I did another search of the shed. I looked

everywhere. And finally …

Yes, yes, yes.

I ran back to the house. 'Dad,' I screamed.

'Look what I've found.'

The Toenail Lisa. Grandad's art.

Dad sort of smiled.

I think.

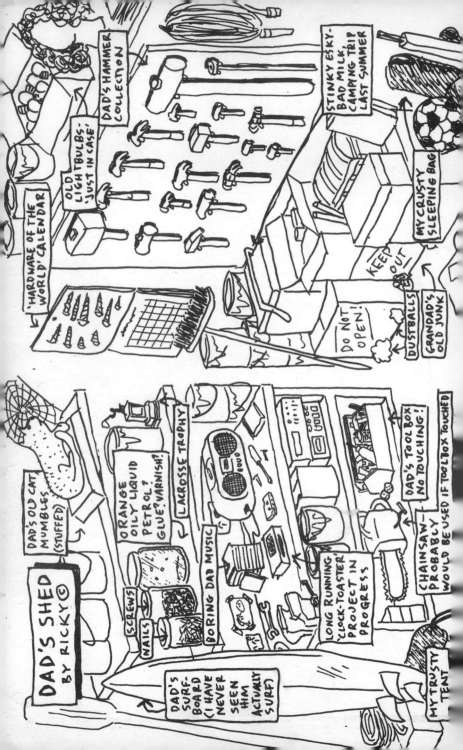